Happy Bi[illegible]!

Because you have roots in Chicago and Pennsylvania, we thought this book was perfect for you!

Love,

Nicholas + Tess

xoxo

The Journey

Sarah Stewart

PICTURES BY David Small

FARRAR STRAUS GIROUX • NEW YORK

CHICAGO

2 INEZ
'RENE
HENRY
SUSIE
LEVI
MARY ESTHER
ERMA JEAN

Distributed in Canada by
Douglas & McIntyre Ltd.
Color separations by
Hong Kong Scanner Arts
Printed and bound in the United States
of America by Berryville Graphics
Typography by Filomena Tuosto
First edition, 2001
1 3 5 7 9 10 8 6 4 2

Library of Congress
Cataloging-in-Publication Data
Stewart, Sarah.
The journey / Sarah Stewart ; pictures
by David Small. – 1st ed.
p. cm.
Summary: A young Amish girl tells her "silent friend," her diary, about all the wondrous experiences she has on her first trip to the city.
ISBN 0-374-33905-8
[1. Amish—Fiction. 2. City and town life—Fiction. 3. Diaries—Fiction.]
I. Small, David, 1945– ill. II. Title.
PZ7.S84985Jo 2001
[E]—dc21 99-31001

HOTEL
FLOWERS

Sunday

Dear Diary,

The luckiest girl on this good earth is writing to you tonight—my birthday—made perfect a few minutes ago by the present of a lace handkerchief. Mother had even hidden a tiny cake in her suitcase! I've never been higher than Aunt Clara's porch, or farther than Yoder's General Store, but this week my dream is coming true. I'm finally in a big city! And more, I've escaped the farm *and chores*! After spending the morning quietly in our room, Mother, her friend Maggie, and I went to the top of one of the tallest buildings in the world. How can I ever thank Aunt Clara for giving me her place on this trip? Well, I'm sure to find a gift for her by the end of the week. But for now, perhaps I'll dream of Aunt Clara and home.

Until tomorrow,
my silent friend,
good night.
Hannah

Monday

Dear Diary,

We spent the entire day walking in and out of stores. I wonder who buys all those things, and *where* do they put them when they get home? We bought hot dogs from a vendor—not at all like eating from the garden. After feeding the pigeons our crumbs, we went into one more store. I was staring at some strange dresses when a saleswoman suddenly held one up to my shoulders. I must have made a funny face, because everyone laughed, even the woman from the store! I wonder if Aunt Clara has finished the dress she was making for me when I left. The fabric is my favorite color—just like the bluest iris. It's late now, and Mother has asked me to turn off our light.

Until tomorrow,
my silent friend,
good night.
Hannah

Tuesday

Dear Diary,

A special day! I know that pride is one of the seven deadly sins, but I can tell you, my silent friend. We were walking in the park when, right in front of us, a horse was startled by a newspaper blowing across his path. My pony can be skittish like that, but I keep a tight rein on him at home. I grabbed the bridle and said, "Whoa, boy, whoa"—like Aunt Clara used to do for me. The driver seemed grateful. Mother, Maggie, and I were treated to a ride around the park with a bride and groom! I just wanted to keep going—I'm not sure *where*.

Until tomorrow,
my silent friend,
good night.
Hannah

Wednesday

Dear Diary,

Today we took a boat ride. All that we've seen from the sidewalks is even lovelier from the water. If I stacked our home, the barn, and my one-room schoolhouse on top of each other, they wouldn't even reach the fourth floor of one of those huge skyscrapers! The city has more of *everything*. More buildings. More cars and buses. More people —all kinds of people—with almost all the colors of a quilt in their different clothes and faces. Going down the street is like making a journey across the whole world. I feel like happiness has rushed up and grabbed me from behind!

Until tomorrow,
my silent friend,
good night,
Hannah

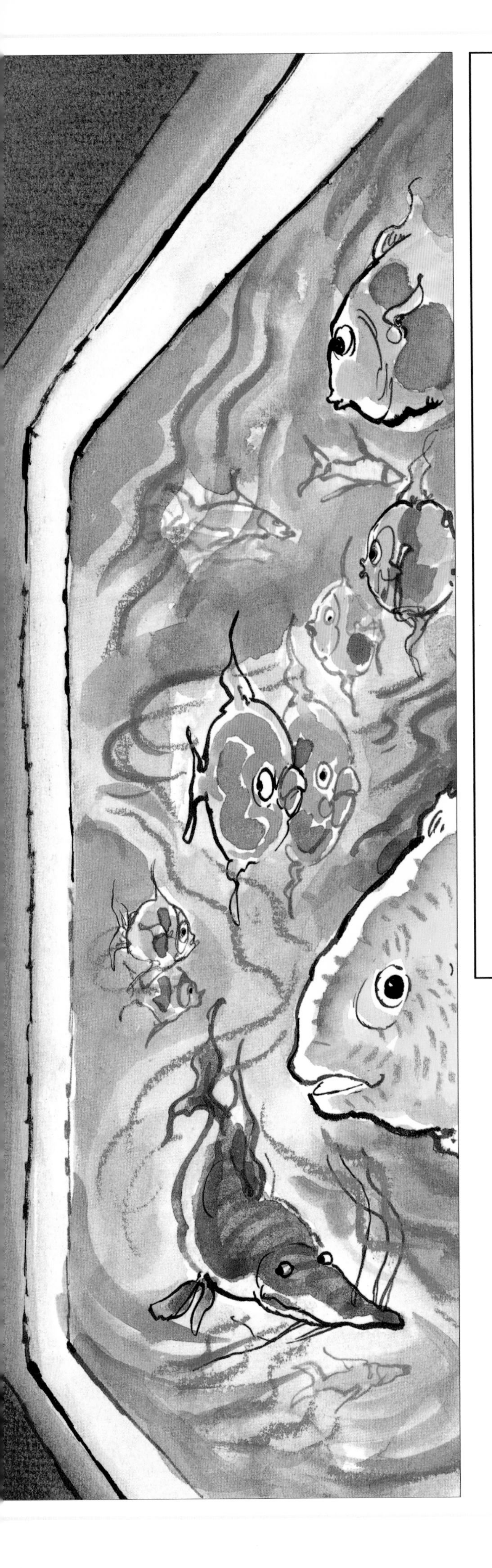

Thursday

Dear Diary,

We went to the aquarium today. There was glass between the fish and me, but at home there always seems to be the *whole lake* between the fish and me when I'm trying to catch one for dinner! I was the center of attention for a moment because I knew the answer to a question that someone asked about the number of oceans in the world. I learned that in third grade. Oops, there's pride sneaking up again. One more thing before I have to turn out the light. I almost bought Aunt Clara a gift today—a huge shell with the waves pounding in it—but the cost was more than all my savings.

Until tomorrow,
my silent friend,
good night.
Hannah

Friday

Dear Diary,

Mother, Maggie, and I wandered around the library this morning, where I was surrounded by my favorite things—books. Then we walked into a great cathedral, and the voices of the practicing choir almost lifted me off my feet. When we've finished singing on Sundays, and the music is still hanging in the air during prayers, sometimes I feel as if I'm going to *fly*! This whole week has been like that! I just don't have the words to equal what I've seen. But I do know this: I felt *larger* when we came back to the hotel this afternoon—not bigger in my body, of course, but in my heart.

Until tomorrow,
my silent friend,
good night.
Hannah

Saturday

Dear Diary,

I cried today, our last morning in this great city, standing in front of a painting at the art museum. No one noticed except Mother. I had to blow my nose on my new handkerchief. I hope Aunt Clara won't think I'm being a big baby when I tell her how much I've missed her and my pony and Dad and Grandma and Grandpa and my sisters and brothers. I didn't think I'd ever miss my brothers! I've written enough poems in my diary this week so that everybody can have one. I'll copy over *two* of my favorite ones as my gift for Aunt Clara, but maybe the best gift to bring home is just myself.

Until tomorrow,
my silent friend,
good night.
Hannah